Bismillah Al Rahman Al Rahim

Ahmad Deen
And the Jinn at Shaolin

by
Yahiya Emerick

New York

Ahmad Deen novels are conceived and written by Yahiya (J.A.) Emerick.

Editing and proof reading provided by:
Reshma Baig and Qasim Najar
Design Consultant: Reshma Baig
Cover Design: Tariq Khan

First print: June 1998

Published and distributed by:
International Books & Tapes Supply
PO Box 5153
Long Island City, NY 11105, USA
Tel: (718) 721 4246
Fax: (718) 728 6108
e-mail: itsibts@aol.com
www.itsibts@aol.com

Manufactured in the United States of America

ISBN 1-889720-02-X

Ahmad Deen

And the Jinn at Shaolin

1

"Ahmad Deen!" Shouted the school teacher. *"Get back in line!"*

"Great." Ahmad whispered to himself. "How am I going to have any *fun* with Ms. Morris around?"

Ahmad looked down at the ticket in his hand. Round-trip airfare for one to China. It still amazed him that he was even here at the airport at all.

But he did it! He was a winner in the essay contest at school and received an all-expense paid tour to see the wonders of Asian culture in, of all places, China itself.

"All passengers on flight 465 to Canton prepare for boarding." Boomed the loud speaker.

Eagerly, Ahmad and the other students in line began to gather their carry-on bags and luggage. Next to the boarding area, Ahmad could see his parents and his sister, Layla, waving excitedly as he moved towards the passage leading to the plane.

He waved back at them and noticed the proud look his parents had on their faces.

"'*Assalamu alaikum!*'" He could see them saying. All the noise and commotion made it impossible to hear them, though. So he simply whispered back, "*Wa alaikum assalam.*"

When the line of students and other passengers reached the door to the plane at the end of a long, sloping ramp, Ahmad could barely contain his excitement.

"This ought to be interesting." Mused Ahmad aloud.

"Yeah," replied someone gruffly from behind him. "*Real* fun. Especially when I get to pound you into *cream cheese.*"

Ahmad turned his head and looked right into the face of his worst nightmare: Brian Stickman. The biggest, most obnoxious bully in the school. Everybody knew he couldn't have been a winner in the essay contest- he didn't have more than three brain cells- but just because his dad's an executive in the school administration, he somehow got in.

"*Hey, Deen!*" Stickman demanded. "I'm in 3B. What seat are you in?"

Ahmad looked up at the ignorant mountain of muscle and thanked Allah that he's been able to avoid this guy all through high school so far, but when he looked down at his seat number, he felt sick to his stomach and replied, "3C."

Stickman laughed and then snarled, "That's a

window seat. I hope there ain't *a problem* if we switch places?"

Ahmad sighed. Not wanting to make a scene he reluctantly replied, "*Naah*. No problem at all."

It was going to be a long flight.

2

"*Hand me another bag!*" begged Stickman to the stewardess as she passed by.

Ahmad grinned in silent satisfaction as he watched the so-called "tough guy" getting sicker and sicker. His face was green, purple and red all at the same time.

The funny thing was that they were no longer in the air but had landed ten minutes ago. Stickman must have broken the record for the longest, most horrible air-sickness in history.

Ahmad, however, spent his eleven hour trip quite a different way. He read the brochures about what the tour group was going to see; he napped a little, and finally, he skimmed through his mini-encyclopedia of Chinese history that his dad gave him just before seeing him off at the airport.

As Ahmad looked out the window and past Stickman's crumpled body, he caught his first glimpse of China. He saw that the airport was built on a long, flat expanse of land surrounded by tall grasses near some outer fences. Beyond these he could see the tall skyscrapers and towering buildings of the city of Canton.

"Well, I guess we're here," he muttered.

"*Ooooooh*." Whined Stickman.

Just then, Ms. Morris came down the aisle and called out in a loud voice, "All right you clowns! Listen up! You may think you're slick back home in your nice, safe school, but this is China. *C-H-I-N-A*, China!"

Ahmad rolled his eyes, "Great. *The lecture.*"

"Now, *everyone* will be assigned a buddy before we leave the plane. There are fifteen students. That means one student will be left over. I'll be the buddy of the left-over student." All the kids squirmed in their seat at the unpleasant thought.

"You will share a room with your buddy, sit together at meals and stick together *at all times*." She pointed her

finger at two students as if to emphasize what closeness meant.

"Okay, when I call out the names of each pair, you will stand up *with* your buddy, get your bags and leave the plane quietly. From there we'll take a bus to the hotel."

As Ms. Morris read the list of names, the students groaned and looked worried. Who would have to be her "*buddy?*"

Ahmad managed to avoid that horrible fate. Ms. Morris picked one of the quiet students. When her name was announced, she whined and looked like she just heard that the Angel of Death was coming for her.

Although Ahmad was saved from a punishment worse than death, for Ms. Morris had the reputation of an old war-horse back at school, he still didn't escape unscathed. Ahmad, as it turned out, was going to be buddies *with Stickman*.

3

"I'll take the top bunk!" proclaimed Stickman.

"Fine," sighed Ahmad, as he wondered what he did to deserve this punishment.

As the two boys were unpacking, Ahmad noticed that Stickman had brought some unusual items. From out of his suitcase came a sling-shot, a bundle of firecrackers, a whoopie-cushion, a package of thumbtacks and some spray- paint.

"What's all that stuff for?" asked Ahmad.

"None of your bee's wax," muttered Stickman, who quickly stashed the loot in the top drawer of his dresser. When he noticed that Ahmad wasn't asking further, Stickman blurted out, "I'm gonna make sure I have some fun on this boring trip."

"*Boring?*" Asked Ahmad. "How can you say '*boring*'? You're in another country. There's so much to do and see and find."

"*Man,* you bookworms are all the same." Grumbled Stickman. "All you want to do is learn. Well, I'm not gonna be a geek like you. I'm gonna..."

Just as Stickman was about to finish, there was a loud knock on the door.

Ahmad, grateful for the interruption, opened it up to find Ms. Morris glaring at him.

"Ahmad Deen!" she said. "You'd better be ready to go for the first tour on time. We leave in thirty minutes."

Then Ms. Morris noticed Stickman in the background and addressed him nicely, "Oh, there you are Brian. How are you today, dear?"

"I'm fine, Ms. Morris." Replied Stickman, in a voice so sweet he was obviously faking.

"Could you please be ready to go in a half an hour?"

"Yes Ma'am." He beamed.

"Good, then I'll see you then." Ms. Morris glared menacingly at Ahmad and then closed the door behind her and left.

"*Ha!*" Stickman boasted. "Morris knows *who* the boss is around here."

Before turning to finish his unpacking, Ahmad thought about how wonderful it would be if school administrators never had their own children in the schools they were in charge of.

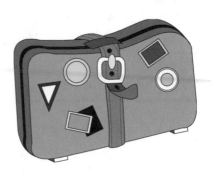

4

They spent the next three days touring museums and hearing presentations by local teachers and professors. Ahmad looked forward to both activities, but Stickman, who had the attention-span of an insect, kept fidgeting and acting stupid.

Once, while they were viewing some samples of *Tang Dynasty* pottery, Stickman took some of his thumb tacks and threw them on the floor. When Ahmad noticed what he was doing, he took it upon himself to quietly pick them up. Another time, when they were eating dinner at the hotel restaurant, Stickman kept grossing everyone out with his tales of what *really* happens in Chinese restaurants.

Ahmad didn't know how much more of this he could take. He didn't even want to make his prayers in the same room as Stickman because he knew the bully would disrupt him, so he made them around a corner in the hallway. Having patience was a constant thing he asked for in his prayers.

On the fourth day, Ms. Morris gathered all the students after breakfast and announced, "Class, today I have a special treat for you. We've been invited to tour the central market of Canton!"

All the students smiled in anticipation. No presentations today and no lectures. They would finally get to see something exciting: the hustling, bustling market of Canton.

Ahmad, too, was happy. He would get some relief from having to suffer sitting next to Stickman in places everyone was supposed to be quiet. With all the distractions and neat things to see there, Stickman would surely have his attention elsewhere. Then Ahmad could get back to what he really enjoyed: seeing, experiencing and learning new things.

5

The bus left the station, leaving Ms. Morris and her students in the middle of the busy downtown markets of Canton. As far as the eye could see, there were tall buildings with little stores on the ground floor of each. In front of the buildings, practically jamming the sidewalks, were little stands, carts and tables full of items for sale. The colors of the whole seen were a mixed jumble, a kaleidoscope almost. There were people all over the place, crowding in the streets and side-walks like ants.

After the students looked for a few moments and tried to take in all the amazing sights, smells and colors, Ms. Morris announced, "Okay, we'll be going in three different big groups. I'll be taking one and the other two will be headed by our hosts from the hotel." Two men who accompanied them on the bus from the hotel came forward.

"This is Mr. Chen." Ms. Morris said, while pointing to the man on her left. "And this is Mr. Wu." She pointed to the man on her right. "Whoever you are with, you will stick by that person. We have six hours in the market today, and after that we'll all meet back here at the bus station. If

I hear anyone gave their guide trouble, then that person will spend the rest of the tour in their hotel room doing worksheets!"

As it turned out, Ahmad and Stickman, along with four other students, were placed with Mr. Wu. He was a nice enough person and spoke passable English.

"Where would...you like to see first?" Mr. Wu asked the group.

"The restaurants." Blurted out Stickman. "I'm hungry."

"I want to go shopping." One of the female students answered. When several of the other students nodded their heads in agreement, Mr. Wu announced they would explore the stores for two hours and then get some lunch.

Mr. Wu took the students to some of the most remarkable things they had ever seen. Open carts, piled high with fish, squid and crabs. Stores filled with clothes, radios, little knick-knacks and baubles. Every thing a person could think of could be found here. Within half an hour, the three girls in the group each had a shopping bag full of stuff.

"I'm bored." Announced Stickman.

"Oh, great." Thought Ahmad to himself.

"There will be a...uh...demonstration in central square in little while." Mr. Wu said. "We will go and watch."

"What are they going to do?" Asked Ahmad.

"They demonstrate...uh...martial arts." Mr. Wu replied.

"All right!" Stickman beamed. *"Bruce Lee!"*

Ahmad snickered to himself and wondered if Stickman could even spell the name he just said. Well, in any case, martial arts were something Ahmad enjoyed as well. This should really be exciting.

6

The show began with a colorful display by each martial arts school doing something called a Lion Dance. It was traditional to open martial arts contests with each school giving its own performance to try and out-do the others.

The students watched in rapt attention as each school sent a team of lion-dancers in the middle of the open park area. The crowds of people who came to watch applauded and cheered as the lion bobbed its head and opened its mouth in a fake roar.

After the lion-dancing ritual was over, the first school sent its students into the center of the make-shift arena. Three men dressed in traditional black kung-fu uniforms arranged themselves with one standing in front of the other two. The crowd hushed itself and waited quietly. After a brief pause, the three men began doing a form from their style.

They raised their arms and turned their bodies throughout the form in a way that resembled a crane. They executed perfect kicks and kept their time flawlessly together as a group.

"What style is that?" Ahmad asked Mr. Wu.

"That is *Won Hop Gar*, or, as you say, *White Crane Style*." He answered.

"*Ho-hum*," sighed Stickman, as he yawned loud enough to annoy the people near him. "This is boring. Where's the fighting? Where's the pain? All they're doing is some dumb kind of dance."

Ahmad looked at Stickman in amazement. How could he *not* see the purpose and beauty in what the martial artists were demonstrating? Was he that much of an ignorant fool? Only Allah knows.

"I must leave for a few moments." Mr. Wu announced. "You children will stay here and watch the show."

"Can I go over to that restaurant on the corner?" Stickman asked Mr. Wu.

Mr. Wu looked where Stickman was pointing and saw that the restaurant was only a short distance away. "Yes," he replied, "but come back here when you've finished eating."

"No problem," Stickman said slyly as he left the crowd and headed towards the street-side foodshop.

Just then, Ahmad realized that it was time to do his prayers. He was combining *Zuhr* and *Asr salat* and the time for *Asr* was leaving fast. [1]

"*Uh*, excuse me." Ahmad called to Mr. Wu, who was turning to go. "Can I go to the washroom and clean up? I have to do something."

Mr. Wu waved his hand quickly, obviously annoyed at the many requests, and then disappeared in the crowd. The other students didn't even notice that Mr. Wu left. The next performance involved a lady doing a difficult weapons form with two long metal hooks of some sort. To the delight of the crowd she leapt, twirled and swung her weapons around with great skill.

---

1 There are five prayers a day in Islam. Their names are Fajr, Zuhr, Asr, Maghrib and Isha. When traveling, a Muslim may combine some of the prayers together and say them at the same time.

Ahmad took his eyes off the show and looked down the street leading away from the park. He thought he saw some restaurants and stores that looked promising. Without waiting he made a hasty retreat from the crowd and began his search for a bathroom or some other place where he could wash for prayer.

There was nothing on the street he was on. Every restaurant he asked in turned him away. "Don't they believe in public rest rooms?" Mused Ahmad.

Finally, he decided to try another street. As he passed by store after store and did his best to avoid the crowds of people who seemed to be walking everywhere. Ahmad began to wonder how so many people could live in one city. He had never seen so many people in his whole life. His father told him that in Mecca, during the *Hajj*, that there were millions of people there. Maybe Mecca looks something like this. [2]

---

2 Once in a lifetime, if he or she is able, a Muslim goes to make a pilgrimage in Mecca. This is called the *Hajj*.

"One day," Ahmad thought, "I'll go on Hajj."

Ahmad woke up from his daydream to find himself on another street. This one was not very crowded and there were few stores. "This will have to be the last one I'll try," Ahmad thought. "And if I can't find water here, then I'll just have to make *tayammum*." [3]

As he neared the end of the street, Ahmad noticed a woman pulling a huge cart behind her. It was filled with buckets, boxes, bricks and other things. Ahmad saw that no one passing by was giving her any assistance.

He immediately felt that he should help her, so he walked over to where she was and motioned for her to stop. At first she looked a little afraid. After all, Ahmad was a foreigner to her. But after Ahmad smiled in a friendly way and motioned with his hands that he wanted to help, she smiled happily and gave him the straps.

Ahmad put the straps over his shoulders and began pulling the cart as he followed the woman down the street. They passed by a few blocks and when they reached the place where the woman had to bring the load, she waved to

---

3 If no water is available to wash for prayer, a Muslim can make "dry wudu" or ablution by passing his or her hands over clean sand or rocks and then passing them over his or her face and arms.

Ahmad that they were finished and that he should put the cart down. Ahmad let the straps drop to the ground as the woman pulled a coin out of her pocket. She smiled and tried to give the coin to him, but he merely smiled and waved his hands in front of him.

When she persisted and wanted to give him the coin, Ahmad pointed upwards with his finger and said, "Allah will reward me."

The woman was silent for a moment and then her face brightened as a thought occurred to her. "Al-lah," she said. And then she pointed further down the street towards a large building in the distance.

Ahmad couldn't quite understand what she was getting at. If she thought Allah lived down the street, then she was very much mistaken. Most probably she didn't know what he meant. When Ahmad turned to go back the way he came, she stopped him and pointed in the other direction towards the far building and said, "Al-lah."

Ahmad, not wanting to disappoint the woman he just helped, decided he would go where she wanted him to and then would try and find his way back to the martial arts demonstration. He waved farewell to the woman who waved back and then set off in the direction of the large building. But unknown to Ahmad, someone else was watching. And that person considered what just happened very carefully.

7

Stickman reached the restaurant after dodging around throngs of people. The extra work made him even more hungry. *"Stupid people,"* he thought, "who do they think they are? I'm dying of hunger and all they want to do is walk around like *snails!"*

The aroma of food reached his nostrils as he looked upon piles of noodles, chicken stir-fry and pastries. "I'll take some of these and those." He told the old woman sitting behind the counter as he pointed. Although she couldn't understand English, she knew what he wanted and piled up a heaping bowl of noodles and chicken.

Stickman dropped a few American dimes in the old woman's hand and started gorging himself on the feast. The old woman looked at him in disgust.

When he had finished his meal, Stickman casually placed the bowl back on the front counter and started to head back to the park. *"How boring,"* he thought, "they need to do some fighting. Whoever heard of a martial arts demonstration where there's *no fighting?"*

Out of the corner of his eye, Stickman noticed Mr. Wu walking through the crowd. He seemed to be headed for an alley-way between two old buildings.

"Where's he going?" Stickman wondered. Without even thinking about the fact that he was supposed to return to the park when he was through, Stickman changed direction and pushed through the crowds following where Mr. Wu had gone.

When he reached the alley, Stickman peered around the corner and saw no one there. He decided to investigate. This would be more fun anyway than that boring *demonstration.*

Stickman walked into the alley and saw old crates and garbage scattered around. Why would Mr. Wu come here? When he reached the end of the alley, it stopped at a brick wall with no way out. "Where did he go?" thought Stickman. "This alley is a dead-end."

Suddenly, a loud grating rumble broke the silence. The brick wall was starting to move. In a panic, Stickman dove behind an old crate and watched in wonder as a section of the brick wall opened up revealing a door behind it.

A moment later, the door opened and out walked Mr. Wu, carrying a small bundle. Mr. Wu paused, turned around and closed the door. Then the false brick wall cover slid back in place, concealing the secret entrance. Stickman stayed as quiet as he could until Mr. Wu passed back down the alley, leaving him alone.

When the coast was clear, Stickman crept cautiously out from behind the crate. He noticed he ripped his pants and frowned angrily. He stood before the brick wall in awe. "A secret passage!" He mused. "Where did it go? Finally, some excitement!"

Immediately, he traced over the bricks with his hands, looking for the hidden catch that must surely open the door. Although his basic nature should have made him afraid, this was just too exciting a situation for him to notice. What would he find? Treasure! Money! Who knows?

After a minute of searching, Stickman's hand felt a small switch behind one of the bricks. Excitedly he pushed it in and stood back as the wall of bricks shuddered and moved aside exposing the door behind it. Without even considering what he was doing, Stickman pulled the door open and stepped inside.

He found himself in a long, well-lit hallway. Large, gray stones were embedded in the floor, walls and ceiling. *"Cool,"* he found himself saying. He began walking carefully, slowly down the passage. After a few steps, an automatic switch activated, closing the door and fake wall behind him. He wasn't too worried, though. There would probably be a switch to open them from the inside as well.

After a few minutes, he came to a fork in the passageway. He could go left or right. Both ways looked identical. He took the left side. After about a hundred feet he came upon a dead end wall with a small wooden door. He put his ear on the wood to see if he could hear anything. Nothing. He reached for the door latch and turned.

When he opened the door he saw three men working at a small table.

The table had piles of white powder on it which the men were scooping up into small containers. Instantly, the three men looked up and saw the foreign boy in the doorway. All at once they yelled in alarm and raced to catch Stickman.

Stickman yelled in panic as he slammed the door shut and ran back down the hallway. *"Aaaaaaah!"* he screamed as he looked back to see the men rushing through the door after him.

He ran as fast as he could and almost missed the turn to go back to the fake door. As he rushed down the right tunnel he saw the three angry men gaining on him. Faster and faster he ran. His lungs burnt with the stinging rush of each breath, and he thought he would collapse and die!

But he reached the door and searched frantically for the secret catch to open it again. He fumbled for a few seconds and found it. The men were almost upon him when he pushed through the door into the dark alley. He tripped and fell flat on his face. He rose to his feet and looked behind him to see the three men coming through the secret door after him.

No matter, he was in the alley now, he could outrun them to the street. But just as he got to his feet to run again, he knocked into what felt like a wall of rock. He fell to the ground and lay there a moment before looking up. Behind him the three men stood with fierce anger in their eyes. In front of him he looked up to see...Mr. Wu!

"*Mr. Wu!*" He cried, "*Save me!* Those men are trying to get me!"

Mr. Wu glared at him and demanded, "*What did you see?*"

"*Huh?*" Whined Stickman.

One of the three men said something to Mr. Wu in Chinese. When he had finished speaking, Mr. Wu lowered his voice and said menacingly, "If they are trying to get you, then I will *give you to them*!"

"*No!*" Stickman blurted out. "Help me! Help!"

"You *stupid boy*." Mr. Wu intoned. "You should never have followed me. Now you will have plenty of time to think about your mistake while I decide what to do with you."

Mr. Wu nodded to the three men who picked Stickman up roughly. As he cried and wailed for help, they took him back into the tunnel, sealing the door up behind them.

Mr. Wu smoothed out his clothes, fixed his jacket and tie and turned to rejoin the students at the demonstration.

8

"What an *awesome* building!" Declared Ahmad aloud, for indeed it was a sight to see. A wall at least fifteen feet high ran along the edge of the sidewalk enclosing the structure behind it. From where he stood Ahmad could see the towering building, decorated in traditional Chinese style, looming up towards the sky. It was three levels high, and each floor had its own reddish colored roof slanting up towards the center. The outer walls were decorated with designs in red, green and gold.

Ahmad walked along the sidewalk and marveled at the wondrous sight. It was obviously a very old example of Chinese architecture. A moment later he came upon a gate leading inside and could see a path surrounded by trees and flower gardens leading towards the main entrance.

"*Allahu Akbar.*" He whispered to himself. Then, he abruptly remembered what he had to do. Prayer time was fast departing. He hadn't prayed a prayer late in so long, and he didn't want to start now.

He looked around himself at the street and the sidewalk. There were only a few people passing by anywhere, so he resolved to make *tayammum* and pray right where he was.

He crouched down and found a clean patch of rock. He made his *niyyah* [4] and was just about to begin when he noticed out of the corner of his eye that some people were coming towards him from down the street. He decided to wait until they passed by, so he stood up and stepped back.

As they came closer, Ahmad could see that there were three men in the group, obviously native dwellers of this city. But something struck Ahmad as strangely familiar. Although they were wearing normal clothes for this part of the world, each man wore a small white hat that looked just like a *kufi*!

But how? Did Chinese people wear *kufis*? Then, Ahmad remembered what he had read in his book about

---

4 *Niyyah*: Intention to do something. Islam requires that every action must be done for the right reason, so Muslims make their niyyah before prayers.

China. There were lots of Muslims here, and their roots went back hundreds of years. Were these Chinese Muslims? Ahmad had to find out.

"*Assalamu alaikum,*" he announced as they were passing by where he stood. [5]

The men stopped abruptly, obviously startled at the words of this foreigner. The oldest among them, an elderly man with a small white beard, smiled slightly and replied, "*Wa alaikum assalam.*"

Ahmad smiled back in relief as the men extended their hands in friendship. After a few moments of exchanged greetings, Ahmad made a gesture from the prayer procedure and said, "I need to make my *Salat.*"

Although the men didn't understand English, they knew what he wanted and eagerly motioned for him to follow them. Ahmad obediently fell in step with them as the men continued down the sidewalk.

Much to Ahmad's surprise and delight the men led him to the entrance of the beautiful building he had been admiring. The four entered the large main gate and passed on the little foot-path Ahmad had seen from the street. On either side of the path were luscious patches of flowers, shrubs and trees. The colorful petals mixed with green leaves made quite a pretty sight. This was a place worth visiting again thought Ahmad.

---

5 The universal Muslim greeting which means, "Peacebe to you." The reply means, "To you be peace."

The three men, with Ahmad following closely, reached the end of the path that led to the main entrance of the building. Ahmad looked up and saw the highest roof stretching far above him. "Beautiful," He whispered. Then he brought his gaze lower and examined the huge front entrance.

There were two massive double-doors with Chinese writing around the outer-frame. In addition, a large, red sign hung over the top of the door that had gold letters woven in an interesting design. It only took a second for Ahmad to register what the sign said. *"La ilaha illa Allah, Muhammad-ar Rasul Allah."* [6] Ahmad was amazed! There, in golden Arabic letters, was the pledge of Islam! "That means that..." Sputtered Ahmad, "...that this is a *Masjid! Allahu Akbar"*

When the three men heard him say that phrase, they nodded their heads and repeated, *"Allahu Akbar."* Then, one of the men pointed to a stone fountain off to the side, and Ahmad instantly knew that was where he could wash for prayer. After he finished his ablutions, the men opened the massive doors and entered a place that Ahmad never knew could exist.

Ahmad followed the men into a huge room that stretched before them in every direction. The floor was covered with rich, red carpet filled with designs. The walls were colored with rich green paint and flower designs were spread all over.

---

6 *"There is no god but Allah, and Muhammad is His Messenger."*

The ceiling went up and up at least two stories above him and was painted with verses from the Qur'an inter-mixed with clouds and nature scenes. The entire place smelled of incense and perfumes.

On the far side of the *Masjid* was a *Mihrab*, or prayer niche, where the *Imam* would stand when he led the prayers.

"*Hai,* Salat." The elderly man said to Ahmad, pulling him from his wonderment. Ahmad took another quick look around him and said dreamily, "I have to make my *Zuhr* first."

The elderly man nodded and the three waited as Ahmad did his shortened *Zuhr* prayer. When that was done, Ahmad joined his new found friends in *'Asr* prayer and the experience, he knew, would stay with him a life-time.

9

Ahmad stayed in the *Masjid,* or *Mosque,* only long enough for the three men to give him a quick tour. They showed him some more of the gardens outside and took him to the small school building in the back of the courtyard.

Ahmad had to leave quickly, however, because he didn't want to make Mr. Wu angry for returning so late. But before parting, the elderly Chinese brother produced a book from one of his pockets and handed it to Ahmad as a gift.

Ahmad took the book in his hands gratefully and exchanged farewell greetings with the men before turning to exit the front gate that led out to the street. He had to hurry. The martial arts demonstration probably ended by now, and he was surely holding everyone up.

Without even looking at what the book was, he tucked it in his jacket pocket and made a hasty retreat. One day he would like to return and spend more time with the wonderful brothers he met here. *"Insha'llah,"* he whispered to himself.

Ahmad retraced his path as fast as he could remember. He noted the landmarks he had passed before and made pretty good time. When he found the street leading back to the park where the demonstration was, he picked up his pace and started to jog. The quicker he returned, the less hot water he would be in.

There were fewer people on the streets now, so Ahmad had little trouble dodging in and out of the carts and little make-shift stores on the sidewalks. Ahead, he could see the tops of the trees that lined the park's outer edge. He would be there in no time now.

But just as he was about to get around the last obstacle, a slow moving cart pulled by two men, Ahmad felt something wrap around his leg. With a crash, he tumbled forward head-first to the ground, nearly knocking the cart over in the process. The two men steadied the cart and yelled at Ahmad who lay on the sidewalk shaking his head. When they put their cart back in order the men continued on as if Ahmad wasn't even there.

"What the..." Ahmad cried out. "What did I trip over?"

Just then a strange looking man came out of nowhere and helped him to his feet. When Ahmad looked up into the man's face, he felt a rush of nervous heat in his forehead.

The man was old and gnarled with time and wore odd looking robes that wrapped around him like a blanket. Before he said anything to him, the man lowered the top of

the staff he was holding and tapped it against Ahmad's leg.

"So this is how I tripped." Muttered Ahmad.

"Who are you?" Ahmad asked, not expecting him to understand English. "Why did you trip me? I'm in kind of a rush."

"*Who* I am is not important." The old man replied, "But what *you* must do *is*."

Ahmad was surprised the man knew English and couldn't think of anything to say in reply. Before he could speak the old man continued, "It is written, '*A heart of gold can seal his fate. A wandering warrior they will take. When the sign of good is in his hand, then in haste rejoice the land.*'"

"What's this all about?" asked Ahmad curiously. "Look, I've got to be somewhere. If you need mone..."

"I have seen," the old man cut him off, "a heart of gold. You helped that woman with her cart when you didn't have to. And you refused any payment in return. When she sent you to the place of the *Hui,* [7] you were taken in by them and made welcome. Those are two of the signs I have searched for."

"*What signs?*" insisted Ahmad, less impatiently this time.

"You have a mission to fulfill. You are the heart of gold we seek. You are the wandering warrior taken in. I know not about *the sign of good in the hand,* but the signs are coming together."

"I still don't understand?" Ahmad replied. "*What mission? What signs?*"

"You must go to the Shaolin temple in Hunan Province. Look for a man named Shang-Dao. Tell him *Hung See Quan* sent you. He will know what to do."

"How can I go there? I'm a student on a school tour. I can't just leave. I'm no warrior either. I've got a room-mate I can't even stand."

The old man raised his hand to silence Ahmad and said in a low voice, "You must go. You will find a way. It is there you will find your companion." Then without speaking further, the old man turned and walked away

---

7 *Hui* is the Chinese term for a Muslim. This comes from the name of the Hui people who are almost all Muslims.

through a crowd of people. He vanished from Ahmad's sight as quickly as he had come.

Ahmad stood in amazement. What was that all about? He didn't know, that was for sure.. But what he did know was that he was really late and would probably have a lot of explaining to do. Ahmad turned himself in the direction of the park and walked the rest of the way in silence.

10

"Ahmad Deen!" Shouted a very, very angry Ms. Morris. "Where have you been?"

Ahmad had returned to the park expecting to find only Mr. Wu and the other kids in his group, but his worst nightmare came back to haunt him: Ms. Morris.

"Who do you think you are running off like that?" She fumed. "You knew the rules, yet you deliberately disobeyed them!"

Behind her stood Mr. Wu, looking annoyed. "I told him to be back very quickly." He said sternly.

Ms. Morris, not even looking back at him, continued, "I knew there'd be trouble with at least *some* of the students. That's why I decided to check up on each of the tour groups. It's a good thing, too."

Ahmad shifted uncomfortably. He could see that the martial arts demonstration was long since over with, and he was indeed in big trouble.

"Now," Ms. Morris demanded, "where is Brian Stickman?"

"I don't know," answered Ahmad, "I went to wash up, and I got side-tracked. He didn't come with me."

"He asked to go to the restaurant on the corner." Mr. Wu said. "After that he didn't return."

"Well, we'll wait here until he returns. How long ago did he leave?" She asked Mr. Wu.

"About two hours ago," he replied.

"Whatever," she huffed. "As for you, *Deen*, you broke the rules, so you're going to spend the rest of the trip locked in your hotel room. You will not go anywhere or see anything more of China for the next ten days."

Ahmad hung his head low. "*Great.*" He muttered. "Just what I needed."

"You brought it on yourself." Announced Ms. Morris, as if she were addressing all the other students gathered. "As soon as Brian returns, your sentence will begin."

"Is Stickman going to get the same punishment?" Ahmad asked, for the idea of two weeks cooped-up with him was not very inviting.

"No," responded Ms. Morris, "I can't trust you two alone together. For the rest of the tour he'll be close by me, in my group, where I can keep an eye on him. Oh, by the way. We're leaving tomorrow for an extended trip to see the Great Wall and won't be back for over a week. I'm sorry, you'll miss that too."

Ahmad wanted to groan in disappointment but decided not to give Ms. Morris the satisfaction. She'll never see him squirm. He's stronger than that. He'll bide his time and play tough.

The group waited for another hour. Then one hour became two and still there was no sign of Stickman. Mr. Wu suggested that maybe he was hopelessly lost and that the police should be called. Ms. Morris, who was getting angrier by the minute, agreed. She would take all the students back to the hotel while Mr. Wu would call the police and ask their help in tracking down the wayward Stickman.

When they returned to the hotel, Mr. Wu escorted each student to his or her room and then left. After Ahmad was deposited in his room, he sat on the bed and thought about his situation. He was going to be stuck in the hotel room for almost two weeks. The rest of the tour was over for him.

Stickman was gone too. Well, maybe that wasn't so bad. But when Ahmad remembered what had kept him from returning to the park on time, he felt a little better. He wouldn't have traded his little adventure for anything.

"Allah knows best," he mouthed, remembering what his father taught him to say in times of uncertainty. Ahmad also knew better than to dwell on what was already passed. He remembered the Sunday school teacher who drilled into him the saying of Prophet Muhammad, *"You should never say 'what if this or what if that.'   Instead you should say, 'Allah has planned. Allah has carried out His plan, and I will be patient.'"*

As he got ready for bed, he mused over his encounter with the Chinese Muslims. They were beautiful people. Then, he remembered the strange old man and what he said. Ahmad drifted off to sleep thinking about golden hearts and wandering old men: Shang Dao, Hung See Quan, signs of good in the hand. It was going to be a long night.

11

Ahmad waited in line at the hotel restaurant for his morning breakfast. He had already showered and got himself dressed in the hope that Ms. Morris would change her mind and let him come after-all. When he received his tray of noodles and rice, Ahmad took it from the hotel employee and thanked him. He then returned to his room, closed the door and started munching on the simple fare.

His meal was interrupted, however, when a loud knock came upon the door. Ahmad wiped his mouth on a napkin and said loudly, "Who is it?"

"Open this door, Ahmad Deen!"

"Oh great." Thought Ahmad, "I can't even enjoy breakfast."

Ahmad opened the door and saw Ms. Morris standing there. She was dressed in traveling clothes and had a hat and jacket on.

"We're getting ready to leave now," She said. "Just thought you'd like to know that Mr. Wu informed me that Brian Stickman still hasn't been found."

Ahmad shifted his weight to his right leg and replied, "Oh."

"We can't hold up the whole tour because one student got lost. So, I've given instructions to Mr. Wu that when he's found, he's to be marched straight to this room where he'll stay for the rest of the trip."

Ahmad felt his breakfast suddenly start to churn in his stomach.

"When he *is here*," she continued, "you two will keep each other company just fine. Oh, don't worry, you won't be bored. I have here a report for you both to work on that'll take at least ten days to finish." She pulled out a stack of papers and handed them to Ahmad. Before leaving she added, "And they'd better be done when we get back."

Ahmad took the papers and sat on the bed. An assignment!

Research Report

What are the Origins of Modern-Day China

Report Length:
16 pages
(Report Based on Enclosed Worksheets)

Stickman to be put in here with him after all? There had to be some over-riding cosmic meaning to all of this. What could possibly go wrong next? Ahmad propped his pillows up against the headboard of his bed and took out his book on China. He thumbed through it and looked up Great Wall. He wanted to know more and this was as good a time as any. He obviously wasn't in a hurry or anything.

A few hours later there came another knock on Ahmad's door. "Uh oh," thought Ahmad, "*Stickman* is here."

But when he opened the door, the only person he saw was Mr. Wu.

"Good morning," Mr. Wu said. "I am here to inform you that we have not found your companion. The police have searched everywhere and are now treating the matter as a, ah...kidnapping. Your teacher has taken the other students on an extended tour, and I will remain here to assist the police in their search. When he is found, I will bring him here. You and your curious friend have caused me much trouble, and I do not appreciate it. You are not to go anywhere, for any reason. Is that understood?"

Ahmad nodded his head slowly and then closed the door and returned to his bed. "*Kidnapped?*" he thought. "*Stickman? Why?*"

12

The whole day passed and still there was no word of Stickman. Ahmad wondered why anybody would want to kidnap *him*. He must have made the wrong person angry for once. Probably serves him right. But what if he was in real trouble? What did that weird old man say? *"You will find your companion there."* Where was there? At the Shaolin Temple.

Ahmad quickly snatched up his China book and looked up Shaolin in the index. When he found the right page he shuffled through the book until he found the entry. It read:

Shaolin Temple- The name *"Shaolin"* signifies *"The Young Forest Temple."* It was built on the side of the Shao Shih Mountain in the fourth century by Emperor Hsiao Wen. Situated in the central province of Hunan, the Shaolin temple was meant to be a center of learning. But it did not become famous until a

Shaolin Temple- China's Kung-Fu Capital

wandering Buddhist monk named Puti Tamo arrived there in the sixth century. He found the monks unable to withstand the trials of prolonged meditation. Therefore, he introduced physical exercises to strengthen them. These exercises became the basis of modern Kung-Fu. Today, there are many Kung-Fu styles which have their origins in Shaolin Temple boxing. Among the most famous martial arts experts to have come from the Shaolin school are Ma Fu Yee, Lon Dao Fai and Hung See Quan.

Hung See Quan! Ahmad looked again to make sure he wasn't seeing things. "That's what the old man said his name was!" he exclaimed aloud. "He said to go to Shaolin temple and find a man named *Shang Dao*. Tell him *Hung See Quan* sent you and then he would know what to do. And I would find my companion there."

Ahmad's heart was racing. It sounded like such a long shot. How would Stickman get to Shaolin Temple? Why would he have been kidnapped in the first place? Was that old man the famous Hung See Quan? Questions rattled through Ahmad's mind as he became more and more excited. Then, he hit upon something: why did Mr. Wu leave the demonstration? He knew he wasn't supposed to leave the kids alone, even for a moment. And if Stickman was kidnapped, why did Mr. Wu call him curious? What did his being curious have to do with his being abducted? How would Mr. Wu know? Something was fishy here and

Ahmad became determined to find out.

Then, he decided on a plan. He would go to the hotel's front desk and ask them to call Mr. Wu to come over right away. One way or another, Ahmad was going to find out what happened to Stickman.

13

While he was waiting for Mr. Wu to arrive, Ahmad gathered together whatever supplies he thought he might need. He took his small book-bag and put in some containers of food he had, a water bottle, a few items of clothing, his small pocket knife and a few other odds and ends.

Then, he went over to Stickman's dresser. He opened the top drawer and saw the odd things Stickman said he needed to have fun on this trip. There was a sling-shot, firecrackers, spray paint, some left-over thumbtacks and a whoopee cushion. Ahmad took all the items except the tacks and stashed them in his bag. On second thought, he might need everything he can find, so he snatched the thumbtacks also.

He had just finished packing when he heard a knock at the door. He quickly stashed the book-bag behind the bed and called out, "Who is it?"

"It's *Mr. Wu*," came the gruff reply.

Ahmad felt a rush of nervousness enter his body. This was it, do or die. But he steadied himself and opened the door to find Mr. Wu standing in the hallway, looking very, very annoyed. He held a small package under one arm.

"Why did you call me here?" he demanded. "I'm a very busy man. What do you want?"

"Oh. Hi Mr. Wu," he responded. "I've got some good news. The man at the front desk told me he received a call from Brian Stickman and that he's on his way back to the hotel right now."

Mr. Wu looked visibly shocked. He seemed to freeze for a minute, and his face almost turned white.

"But that's *impossible*," he stammered. "Stickman is at..." then he caught himself and calmed down.

"That's not possible," he began again, "because the police would have called me first if they found him. Now, if you're done with your little prank, I've got business to attend to."

With that said, Mr. Wu turned around and walked back down the hallway towards the hotel lobby. Ahmad wasted no time in grabbing his bag and slipping on his jacket. He felt a bulge in his jacket pocket and remembered that the book the Chinese Muslims gave him was still there. "Oh well," Ahmad thought, "no time to take it out now. I'm in a hurry."

Ahmad peered out the door and saw that Mr. Wu had passed around the corner. Seeing his chance, Ahmad stepped into the hallway, quietly closed the door and headed in the direction that Mr. Wu went. When he finally reached the lobby, he barely caught a fleeting glimpse of Mr. Wu walking out the front entrance onto the street. He seemed to be in a hurry and was moving quickly.

Ahmad followed after Mr. Wu as best he could. The elusive man made his way through several different city streets causing Ahmad to wonder where they could be headed. It was mid-day now and the crowds of people were thick everywhere.

Twice Ahmad thought he lost the trail, but then he would manage to see Mr. Wu ahead somewhere. He quickly would regain his prey.

Once Mr. Wu stopped and looked behind him, as if he sensed someone there. When Ahmad saw him turning around, he ducked behind a bunch of people who were looking at a jewelry stand. When Mr. Wu continued on his way, Ahmad came out and resumed his mission.

After another few streets, he saw Mr. Wu round a corner and enter a small, dark alley. By the time Ahmad reached the entrance to the trash-filled corridor, Mr. Wu was already pushing the door in the secret entrance and entering into the passageway. Ahmad barely had time to see what happened before the false brick covering slid back into place, covering the door behind it.

"What's behind that secret door?" Ahmad whispered softly to himself. Maybe it would hold the clue to what happened to Stickman. But how did Mr. Wu fit into all of this? He had to know! Ahmad wasted no time and rushed to the false brick cover.

He searched for the secret lever that he knew must be there and found it in a snap. When he flicked the hidden switch, the wall shuddered and moved away. Ahmad carefully opened the secret door and slipped inside.

He found himself in a long passageway covered in stonework. Seeing that no one was there, he moved down the corridor until he came to a crossing. Left or right, which way? While he considered, he heard the sound of voices coming from down the right tunnel. He quietly headed towards the sounds until he came upon a large wooden door. It was partly open so he had to be careful not to be seen.

When he peeked through the edge of the door, he saw Mr. Wu seated at a large desk. In front of the desk were three men who held their heads low as if they were being yelled at. Mr. Wu was speaking angrily in Chinese and appeared to be scolding them. Every so often he threw in a few English words, and Ahmad began to piece together some of what he said.

"You (something, something) that (something) American boy! (something) room mate (something) called me. (something) said (something) to the hotel. I (something) told you to take him to (something) Shaolin."

One of the three men replied, "We did (something) take (something, something) to Shaolin."

When Ahmad heard the key word, Shaolin, he knew Stickman must be there. But why would Mr. Wu kidnap Brian Stickman? What did he do that was so bad? Ahmad listened for more.

"I will go there now," Mr. Wu said, "to (something) he's still there and (something, something) *take care of him*. While I'm gone, (something) get (something) ready to go. Our buyers (something)."

When Ahmad felt he heard enough, he crept silently away from the door and made his way back to the crossing in the tunnel. He was about to take the way leading back to the secret entrance, but something tugged at him to go and explore the other tunnel. He decided he had a few minutes at least, so he went down the tunnel leading to the left.

After walking a little ways he came to a dead-end. In the wall in front of him was a small wooden door. Ahmad listened for a minute and heard nothing, so he opened the door slowly and peered inside. He saw a table with piles of white powder and small brown packages stacked up in the corner. Next to the table were three stools, obviously for the three men to use when they worked. Quickly, he entered the room and approached the table for a closer look.

He poked at the powder, smelled it, tasted it. It sure wasn't sugar! It looked like some kind of drug or something.

"Cocaine." He whispered to himself.

Ahmad thought about what to do for a minute and then decided on a novel plan. He took out the can of spray paint he got from Stickman's dresser and opened the brown packages which seemed ready for shipment. He sprayed a little paint inside each one, ruining the contents, and then carefully sealed the packages back up to hide what he had done.

When he had finished, he sprayed the surface of each stool with a load of paint, so it remained drippy and wet. Next, he took one of the brown packages and stuffed it in his bag. Finally, he took some thumb tacks from his bag and found a box near the door to hide behind. Patiently, he waited.

He didn't have to wait long, however, for only a few minutes later he heard the sounds of footsteps approaching the door. Ahmad's heart began to beat faster. A moment later the footsteps stopped in front of the door. The door handle turned. Ahmad's forehead started to sweat.

"This had better work," he whispered to himself.

The door swung open, and the three men entered the room. They were mumbling to each other and failed to notice Ahmad hiding behind a crate near the door. Knowing that they had a deadline to beat, the trio rushed to the table, and each took his seat. They began to work, filling the little packages with the white powder.

While they were distracted, Ahmad crept out from behind his hiding spot. He spread the tacks on the floor in front of the door and when that was done, he opened the door as quietly as he could. He looked back at the men who were unaware of the motion behind them and he yelled at the top of his lungs, "**Hey, you!**" Then, he slammed the door shut and ran as fast as he could for the exit.

The three men all jumped up at once in fright. They were taken completely by surprise and were nearly startled out of their wits. Within seconds they were racing for the door to try and catch the intruder. But the second they reached the tacks they let out yells of pain. The sharp little points pierced right through their shoes causing two of the men to fall in the middle of the pointy danger zone.

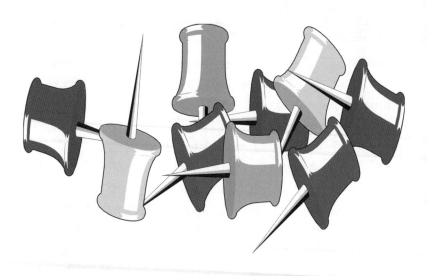

By the time they got through the door, Ahmad had already opened the secret entrance and was running into the alley.

The leader of the three men told the others to take their tack-infested shoes off and get after the intruder. As they ran down the corridor in their stockinged feet, they tripped over each other and barely managed to pick up speed.

One of the men noticed a bright splotch of paint on the pants of his two companions and checked his own pants to see if he had one too. Sure enough, his hands touched sticky, wet paint which made him even angrier. "*Get him!*" he cried as they reached the secret entrance.

Meanwhile, Ahmad ran out of the alley and searched frantically for a policeman. He looked out upon throngs of people walking by, but an officer was not to be seen anywhere. He looked behind him in the alley and could see the three men coming out of the secret entrance after him. They didn't even bother to close it behind him.

"Where are the police when you really need them!" thought Ahmad.

Then Ahmad saw them: four Chinese policemen standing next to a pastry cart a little ways down the street. Wasting no time, Ahmad took the drug package out of his bag, ripped it open a little and poured some of the powder on the street. It was no longer all white, however, as the paint he had sprayed in it earlier had changed the color to an orange-yellow ick. He had to hurry, though, because the three men were already half-way down the alley and coming fast.

Ahmad turned to where the policemen were and shouted at the top of his lungs, "Help! Help! Drugs!"

Ahmad waved his hands in the air like a maniac and shook some of the powder in the air. The police officers, and a good number of other people, looked at the wildly shouting foreign teenager. Seeing trouble, the officers dropped what they were looking at and raced to the source of the noise.

Ahmad dropped the package on the ground and stepped back as the three men rushed out of the alley and pounced in his direction. Ahmad pushed one of the men aside and managed to dodge another one.

The third man grabbed the package off the ground and was about to join the struggle when he looked up into the face of four large police officers. *"Uh oh,"* he said to himself.

When the other two men saw the police, they tried to run but they were quickly nabbed and restrained by the officers nearest to them.

Ahmad pointed to the drug bag and then at the man holding it and said loudly, *"Drugs!"*

When the police officers saw that each of the men had paint on their clothes and that it matched the paint on the cocaine, they immediately started putting hand-cuffs on them. Ahmad then pointed back down the alley at the secret entrance and repeated again, "Drugs!"

When the officers saw the secret entrance in the distance, one of them called on his radio for back-up. Ahmad smiled in triumph and knew he had won this round, but would he be so lucky next time? "Thank you, Allah." He whispered.

The police had the situation well in hand, so Ahmad went to the senior looking officer and said, "American student, Stickman."

Then, he pointed to the three drug dealers now kneeling with their hands cuffed behind their backs. But the officer just looked at Ahmad without understanding, and then shooed him aside so he could concentrate on sending his men into the secret lair at the end of the alley.

"*Great*," whispered Ahmad. "Even if I asked them to help, how long would it take for them to get organized? Would any of them even understand English?"

Then, it dawned on him: Mr. Wu probably never reported Stickman's absence to the police at all! He simply fooled Ms. Morris and said he did. With his teacher away and knowing that Mr. Wu was on his way to *take care* of Stickman, Ahmad decided to go to Shaolin alone. Didn't the old man say he had to go, and that he would find a way? It seemed to Ahmad that the way was made.

Without further thought, he disappeared back into the crowd and headed for the nearest bus station.

14

Ahmad found a bus station and managed to find a ticket agent who spoke at least broken English. When Ahmad told him he wanted to get to Hunan Province to see the Shaolin Temple, the man smiled, slightly amused, and handed him the ticket.

It didn't cost much in American money, so while he waited for his bus to arrive, Ahmad bought some food at a nearby restaurant and munched in silence. Then, he made *wudu* [8] in the station's washroom and found a place to pray.

A half an hour later, his bus came, and Ahmad boarded and took a window seat. To pass the time, he pulled out his China book and used the map to figure out that he had at least a three-hour ride ahead of him.

As the bus left Canton, Ahmad watched the scenery change from urban confusion to rolling farmland. For as far as the eye could see, wheat fields, rice fields and corn fields stretched in all directions. "Not much different from home." He thought.

---

8 *Wudu* means to wash for prayer.

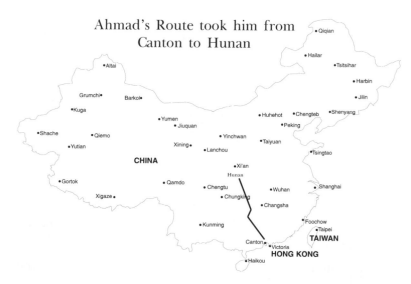

Ahmad's Route took him from
Canton to Hunan

There was only light traffic on the road, so the bus made pretty good time. Along the way, Ahmad managed to doze a little to refresh his wits. He needed to regain his strength after such an eventful day. What, he wondered, still lay ahead of him? Time would tell.

After two-hours they crossed over a brown-colored river that looked like a giant mud flow. It was the mighty Yang-Tze, or Yellow River, which meandered its way over half of China before dumping its silty waters into the East China Sea.

When the bus finally arrived in Hunan Province, it entered a small, bustling village that was built in the shadow of a tall, forested mountain. Ahmad left the bus station quickly and made his way into the center of town, hoping to find out where the Temple was from here. He asked around, but either the people didn't understand English, or they didn't want to help him. He couldn't say for sure.

The daylight was waning, and Ahmad wondered what he was going to do for the night. "There must be some kind of an inn or hotel here," he thought. As he was passing down a street that looked like it may hold promise, he spied something peculiar: Ahead of him stood two odd-looking men loading a cart full of vegetables.

They both wore bright yellow robes and had shaved heads. Ahmad had seen enough Kung-Fu movies to know that these had to be temple monks. Ahmad instantly changed course to go and meet them.

When he approached the monks, who were busy strapping the contents of their cart securely, he waved his hand in greeting and said, "Hey, do either of you speak English?"

The two men looked up at him mutely and then went back to work. "I guess you don't." Ahmad muttered.

The two men finished tying down the vegetables and picked up the front ends of their cart, dragging it behind them as they walked away from the vegetable stand. "Hey, wait a minute," Ahmad called after them. "I need to go to the Shaolin Temple. I have to find my room-mate."

The monks ignored him and kept walking. Ahmad followed behind and thought desperately for something to say that would make them understand what he wanted. They had to take him to the Temple, or his trip would have been for nothing!

Finally, Ahmad remembered what the old man had told him to say, *"Look for a man named Shang Dao. Tell him Hung See Quan sent you."*

"Shang Dao," Ahmad announced. The two monks stopped in their tracks and listened.

"Hung See Quan." Continued Ahmad.

The two monks turned around to face Ahmad with disbelief in their eyes. He met their gaze and pointed to himself saying, *"Ahmad Deen."*

The monks didn't seem to understand his name, but the words Ahmad said before obviously had meaning for them as shown by their surprised expressions. One of the monks started untying the vegetables while the other grabbed a folded sheet from the side of the cart.

The first monk took a bunch of the vegetables in his arms and sat them down on the side of the road. That left just enough space for Ahmad to fit on the cart. The monk motioned for him to get on. When he was settled in, the second monk took the sheet and hid Ahmad under it. Then, they picked up the cart and continued on the dirt-road leading out of town and up into the forested mountain.

"Alhumdulillah." Thought Ahmad. *"Praise Allah. A way in."*

15

The monks walked for about three miles before bringing their cart to a halt. One of them uncovered the sheet that was hiding Ahmad to show him where they were headed. Ahmad stared in wonder as he looked ahead at the massive Shaolin Temple.

The building was at least six stories tall with many sloping angles jutting out from the top. All around it were smaller buildings and walled-in court-yards and terraces.

The mountain-side surrounding the complex was covered in beautiful pine trees, and the setting sun made the whole scene look unreal with reds and purples spread across the evening sky. Ahmad was struck with awe.

The monk who uncovered him interrupted his thoughts, however, by motioning for him to keep quiet no matter what. Ahmad nodded his head; and the monk draped the sheet over his head once more.

Ahmad felt the cart move again and steadied himself as best as he could. A few minutes later the wheels of the cart reached pavement, and he could tell they were probably at the front gate of the temple grounds.

The cart came to a halt as the two monks stopped and let it down abruptly. Ahmad could hear voices talking. At the risk of getting caught, Ahmad decided to see if he could snatch a peek at what was going on.

Slowly, he moved one edge of the sheet away until he could barely see out with one of his eyes. What he saw astounded him.

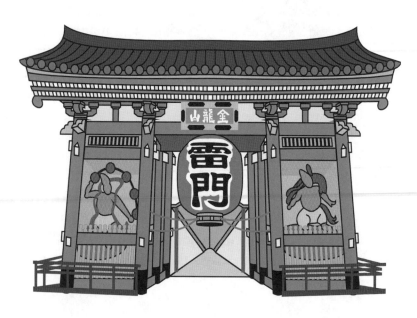

The two monks stood off to the side as four heavily armed men wearing black and gray clothing questioned them. Each of the four men held a large knife and looked like they were ready to use them at a moment's notice. The leader of the men pointed to the cart and the monk replied in Chinese.

"Who are those men, and why are they here at the Shaolin Temple?" Ahmad wondered.

When the lead man seemed to be satisfied, he motioned for the monks to go. Quickly, they returned to the cart and dragged it in through the gates. Ahmad had no clue as to why armed guards stood at the Temple's entrance or why the monks seemed to be afraid of them.

As the monks steered the cart through the first courtyard, Ahmad peeked out again to see colorful monks moving about silently on their individual errands. But they each seemed worried as if some collective fear dominated their thoughts. Ahmad caught sight of a couple of armed guards standing in a tower. What was going on?

The two monks took the cart into a small back entrance to one of the smaller buildings and closed the two large wooden doors behind them. One of them came and helped Ahmad off the cart while the other went ahead through a small passageway leading further into the building. Ahmad was about to ask what was going on when the monk with him again motioned him to be silent.

After a few minutes, the second monk returned and waved for them to follow him down the corridor. Ahmad let himself be led further into the temple complex and was surprised at how gloomy the place was. The passage was dimly-lit and had brick walls and a stone floor. Hardly the kind of place he would want to spend a lot of time in.

After a few twists and turns, the monks stopped in front of a small doorway. The first monk knocked three times, slowly. A moment later the latch turned, and the door swung inward with a slight creak.

Ahmad felt a little nervous. What awaited him on the other side of the door? Was this a trap? Would they close the door on him and lock him inside? Who could he trust? The assault of uncertain feelings caused him to hesitate. Should he go in, or should he run now while he has the chance and get back to Canton?

"No!" he thought. "I came this far already because someone needs my help. There's no turning back now."

Saying a quick "*Bismillah*" Ahmad stepped through the doorway into a small room lit only by a few candles on the far wall. The monks closed the door behind him, and Ahmad almost thought he was tricked until he noticed the man standing in the shadows across from him.

"Who are you?" asked Ahmad.

"The question is," the man responded in a low eerie voice, "why are you here?"

"I'm looking for my room-mate. I believe he is hidden here at the Shaolin Temple. A drug dealer kidnapped him."

"There are many here who are not allowed to leave," the man replied ominously. "Why should you expect him to be alive?"

"He has to be!" stammered Ahmad. "I don't really like him myself, but I'm on a mission to save him and bring him back with me."

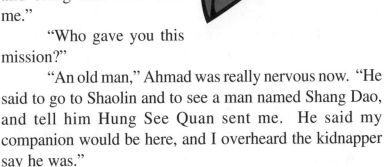

"Who gave you this mission?"

"An old man," Ahmad was really nervous now. "He said to go to Shaolin and to see a man named Shang Dao, and tell him Hung See Quan sent me. He said my companion would be here, and I overheard the kidnapper say he was."

The man stood silently for a moment as if he were considering important matters. Then, he came out of the shadows and announced, "I am Shang Dao. Whoever Hung See Quan sends is welcome here."

Ahmad sighed in relief as Shang Dao opened a door near him and bid him to follow. As they walked down a narrow corridor leading to another room, Shang-Dao asked Ahmad his name. When Ahmad told him, the man simply commented on how strange his name was for him to pronounce.

When they reached the next room, Shang-Dao and Ahmad entered and sat down at a small table near the back wall. A moment later, a monk entered carrying a tray of food and tea which he sat down near the two and then left.

"The criminal of which you speak, would it be *Wu Shou Chi?*"

"Mr. Wu!" Ahmad exclaimed.

"Yes," replied Shang-Dao. "He is an evil man. He sells drugs which harm people and destroy lives."

"Why did he bring my room-mate here to the Shaolin Temple," inquired Ahmad, "and why are all those armed men around?"

"It is a sad tale. Two years ago, Wu Shou Chi was looking for the perfect hide-out for his drug operations. He tried a number of places but barely managed to keep ahead of the law. Once, while he was on the run from the police, he came to the temple looking for sanctuary. We did not know who he was, so we let him in and fed him for a few months."

Shang-Dao paused for a moment while he poured some tea into two small cups. He offered one to Ahmad who accepted it gratefully. Then, he continued his story.

"Wu must have noticed that the police never come here, as we are religious men, so he approached the chief Abbot and told him he wanted to move his crime headquarters here. The chief Abbot refused, and Wu left vowing to return and take over."

"We didn't hear anything from him after that and we thought he disappeared. But one day he returned with a truckload of hired men and demanded to be let in. We refused to open the front gates, and when he sent some of his men to open them, we used our Kung-Fu skills to send them back in confusion."

Ahmad leaned forward and listened more intently.

"He was no match for our warrior-monks, who spend their whole lives training as a part of their daily duties here at the temple. Apparently he knew that too. After a few minutes he brought out a little old man and called up to us on the walls. He said that if we didn't surrender and let him use our temple for cover, he would defeat our Kung-Fu with terrible magic."

"We didn't believe him, so he whispered something to the old man who started waving his arms and chanting something. A few minutes later the ground shook and a flash of light erupted in front of the gates that sent a shiver of fear through the monks. Then, when the light was gone, a huge reddish colored man appeared who stood over seven feet tall! He was an evil spirit summoned by the old sorcerer. Before we could react, the spirit smashed the gates in and the armed men rushed at us and beat us with huge sticks. The spirit somehow made us too afraid to fight back."

"That sounds like some kind of an evil *jinn*! They're demons!" Exclaimed Ahmad.

Shang-Dao appeared distressed for a moment; then he regained his composure and finished his account by saying, "After that we had to do what Wu ordered. He moved his drug headquarters here, and we monks have to go about our business as if nothing was wrong. We don't dare fight him or his men, for the demon, who calls himself *Xandar Kul*, is here in the lowest levels of the main temple, waiting to come out whenever Wu calls. Until the demon is removed, we are powerless."

Shang-Dao pointed towards the food on the table and motioned for Ahmad to eat. Although he was ravenously hungry, Ahmad resisted the urge to gobble up everything in sight and merely took a few small bites and tried to work up a response to the fantastic story he just heard.

"But why would Mr. Wu kidnap *my* room-mate?" Ahmad asked. "I mean, we're just students on a group tour."

"Maybe your companion saw or heard something he shouldn't have."

Then, Ahmad remembered that Stickman left the martial arts demonstration around the same time Mr. Wu did. Ahmad nodded his head slowly. Stickman probably saw whatever it was that Mr. Wu was doing when he left and got nabbed. It was so much like Stickman to poke his nose where it didn't belong.

"The old man who sent me here told me a riddle. I still don't know what it means."

"Ah," Shang-Dao responded, "before Wu could gain

complete control over the temple, one of the old monks, Hung See Quan, had a daring idea. He said he would look for someone who could help us. He told us a strange riddle. Then, he slipped away in the night vowing never to return until he found his goal."

"He told an odd riddle to me," Ahmad said. "And he said that I fit the person in the riddle and that the mission was mine. But I don't understand what it means."

Ahmad tried to remember what the old man had told him. Finally, the memory of that strange incident flooded back upon him and he recited, *'A heart of gold can seal his fate. A wandering warrior they will take. When the sign of good is in his hand, then in haste rejoice the land.'*

"He explained the first part to me: he said it was when he saw me help someone and not take any reward for it. The second part, he said, was when some new Muslims I met made friends with me. The other two parts I don't know yet, but the lines also called me a warrior. I took a little martial arts here and there, but I'm no warrior."

Shang-Dao looked upon the youth thoughtfully for a moment. Then he answered in a low voice, "If you are the one who was sent, I will not argue. I will send some monks to quietly try and locate where your friend is being held. In the meantime, you may not be a warrior now, but that can be changed.

"Starting tomorrow you will begin training in Shaolin Kung-Fu. You will spend each day with our master instructors who will give you a fast course in the techniques you will need to help you. I still don't know what we will do about Xandar Kul, but at least you will be more ready to rescue your friend and get him away from here."

Shang Dao then stood up and looked upon Ahmad gravely. "You will be pushed hard. Harder than you ever thought possible. Prepare yourself. You will sleep here. Gather your strength. Tonight you rest, but tomorrow is another day."

With that said, he turned around and retreated from the chamber, closing the door behind him.

Ahmad was left alone. It was probably dark outside by now. Ahmad was grateful he had the evening to consider and think over all that he was told. He would be awake for a while. Looking at the tray on the table made him remember his hunger and he reached for more food until he had his fill.

He found a water jar in the corner where he washed for prayer. After he finished his combined *Salat*, he lay on a small mat he found and thought long into the night. *"Tomorrow is another day."* Then, he fell asleep.

16

Ahmad was awakened early by the sound of thumping on his door. "Ten minutes," a voice boomed from outside.

He sprang up from the uncomfortable mat he had slept on and went to the water jar where he splashed cold water on his face. After he finished washing, he made his morning prayer and slipped on a new shirt he had in his bag. He also found a pair of sweat-pants lying on the stool next to the table. They must have been placed on the table in the middle of the night while he was asleep. There was also a small tray of rice and vegetables.

Ahmad barely finished the last bite before the thumping sound came again upon the door. "Come out!" a voice bellowed.

Ahmad opened the door and saw a large, burly man standing in the corridor. He wore the orange robe of a monk and carried a short, thin stick about two feet in length.

"I am Master Chai." He said. "I will come at this time every morning to teach you strength. Do whatever I say without hesitation. Follow me."

Without waiting for Ahmad's reply, the monk turned around and walked down the passageway. Ahmad had to step quickly to catch up with him and then fell in place behind him. A few minutes later Master Chai led Ahmad into a large room filled with an assortment of weights, bars and other items he couldn't identify.

"Stand here," Chai pointed to a spot near the center.

"A man who would be *a warrior* must have strength and endurance. Weak arms and legs mean weak techniques."

Ahmad listened as the instructor pointed to the different machines and explained each one's purpose. Then, after showing Ahmad some basic warm-up exercises, Master Chai took some odd looking rings out of a cabinet.

He gave them to Ahmad and told him to put the iron rings on his wrists and on his ankles. When he put the heavy weights on he found that he could barely lift his arms or legs. Chai escorted Ahmad into an adjoining room where a small muddy pool lay in the center of the floor.

"*Get in.*" Ordered Master Chai. Ahmad obeyed and let himself down into the water. The sides of the pool were steep and there were no hand-holds, so Ahmad slid right in. When his feet touched the bottom, the water was up to his neck.

"Now climb out." Master Chai demanded. With the heavy weights on his arms, Ahmad had a lot of trouble leaving the pool. When he finally climbed onto the floor, he collapsed tiredly.

"Now get in again," Master Chai said. Ahmad did as he was told only to have to climb out once more. He would enter and exit the pool many times. After two hours Ahmad thought he was going to drop from exhaustion.

Finally, Master Chai said, "Enough for today. Tomorrow, you will carry stones." Ahmad, who was sweating profusely, fell down and felt his tired muscles tingle. Then, he was escorted to a small courtyard where a refreshing pool of water was made available for him to bathe in. When Ahmad finished his quick dip, he found fresh clothes waiting for him on a stone bench. He slipped on the sweat pants and light shirt and was taken back to his room where he instantly lay on the mat and took a much needed nap.

A little while later, he was awakened by the sound of tapping on his door. This time he found a slender, elderly monk waiting for him in the hallway. "I am Master Lui." He said. "I will come everyday at this time to teach you to have fast reflexes and accuracy. Do not hesitate to do my bidding. Follow me."

Ahmad followed Master Lui who led him up a flight of stairs and down a long, stone corridor to a different training room. This one had candles atop metal stands, rings hanging from the ceiling, clay pots stacked up in a corner and incense sticks burning slowly near the corners of the room.

"Stand there." Ordered Master Lui. "A man who would be a warrior must have quick reflexes and great accuracy. A slow fighter who misses his targets will lose every battle."

After explaining what each training exercise was for, Master Lui put Ahmad to his first task. He made him stand between two hot incense sticks. Each one was pointed directly at Ahmad's cheeks and was only about an inch away from his face on either side. Then, Master Lui sat on a high table a little ways in front of Ahmad and took out a chain with a ball on the end. He held one end of the chain in his hand and let the ball swing back and forth, suspended at the bottom.

"Follow the moving ball with your eyes," he said, "but do not move your head."

Ahmad, realizing that if he turned his head at all he would be burned on the cheeks, nodded slightly that he understood. As the ball moved back and forth gently, Ahmad turned his eyes left and right. The smell of the burning incense made his eyes water a little, but it was no great discomfort.

"This is going to be easy," thought Ahmad.

A moment later, Lui started moving the ball faster, so Ahmad had to move his eyes faster.

Suddenly, without warning, Master Lui caught the ball as it passed on the right, stopping it abruptly. Ahmad's natural reflexes made him twitch his face to the right, and a hot burning sensation shot through his cheek as his face hit the smoldering incense. "Ow!" he cried, as he raised his hand to his cheek.

"I told you *not to move your head*," chided Master Lui. "Begin again."

The next round began with Ahmad moving his eyes to follow the swinging ball. But this time, when Lui stopped the ball, Ahmad held his head still. "Good," Master Lui exclaimed.

After another hour of various tests, including hitting small clay pots through hanging rings and dodging small stones thrown at him, Ahmad was again escorted to his room where he collapsed on the mat and rested.

The third instructor, Master Yu, came and announced that he was to teach Ahmad fighting techniques. With him, Ahmad began to learn the Shaolin Long-Fist form and the applications of each move. This class was by far the longest, lasting at least four hours. Master Yu explained that it would take at least five days to learn the basic fighting

form and a few more to study the most important combat elements within it. When they were through for the day, Ahmad was again taken back to his room where fresh food awaited him.

Later, as the afternoon wore on, Ahmad was visited by a fourth and final instructor, Master Fong. He took Ahmad to a chamber that had wooden poles of various sizes placed haphazardly around the place.

After explaining that a fighter had to be aware of everything around him, Master Fong pressed a lever that started the poles spinning slowly.

"Every pole has a round button on it," he said, "and the only way to stop each pole is to hit that button. Do not think of it as easy, for tomorrow I will add the wooden arms to the spinning poles that you must dodge. Begin."

Ahmad ran through the spinning poles and tried his best to hit the buttons as he was told. But it was hard to hit them as the poles didn't stay stationary. When he did get lucky and hit a button, causing that pole to stop, Master Fong merely yawned and said, "Try harder."

After an hour of this training, Ahmad was returned to his room where he prayed and then slept as soundly as he ever did in his whole life. When the next morning came, again, Ahmad heard the loud thumping on his door: *"Ten minutes!"*

17

Over a week passed before Ahmad received word of where Stickman was being held. During a training session with Master Lui, Shang Dao entered the chamber and asked to see Ahmad alone. Master Lui agreed to end the day's training early and exited through a side door.

Once they were alone, Shang Dao looked at Ahmad carefully. His muscles were toned, his stance was light and his eyes seemed sharper and more focused. "You have been training hard." he said.

Ahmad humbly nodded and replied, "I'm trying my best."

"You're *best* will be needed," Shang Dao continued, "for your moment is at hand. I have talked with your teachers, and although they would like to continue your training for quite some

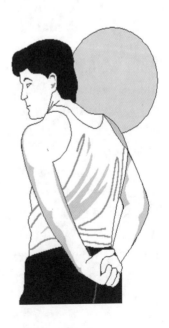

time, they have all agreed you have been an able student and have learned things quickly.

"Since the time you've arrived, you have increased your strength, reflexes and fighting abilities. Master Yu even tells me you have learned the entire Shaolin Long Fist form and understand many of its combat applications. That's an impressive achievement."

Ahmad, who was too tired to feel overly-proud, merely smiled and said, "I still need to learn so much more. My teachers have shown me that I barely scratched the surface in Kung-Fu."

"That is true, yet the time for action has come. One of our monks has learned where your companion is being held. *Brian* is his name, I think."

Ahmad nodded affirmatively.

"We had difficulty locating him because Wu Shou Chi arrived about the same time as you did and moved the boy to an area monks are not allowed in: a place near Xandar Kul. We have also learned that Wu is planning to silence the boy forever. We must move fast, or he will die."

Ahmad shifted his weight and felt a rush of adrenaline course through his body. "When do we get him?" he asked.

"Tomorrow night," Shang Dao began, "we shall begin. Wu will be out of the temple inspecting some fields of cocaine near a village down the way. While he is gone, we will act. I will come for you when it is time. Return to your chambers and rest now, for tomorrow you may need every strength you can muster."

Shang Dao then retreated from the chamber, closing the door behind him. Ahmad looked around the room for a moment. He smelled the incense burning nearby and felt as if time was about to stop, leaving him to enjoy the simple life of a Kung-Fu student. He would miss this experience- if ever he got out of this alive.

He slowly came back to his senses, however, and casually returned to his own room. As usual, a tray of food and a change of fresh clothes awaited him. After eating and doing his prayers, Ahmad sat down on his mat to think.

He ran over in his mind all the events that had brought him to this strange new world: The essay contest, the airport, Ms. Morris and her "Buddy" system, the Masjid and the Chinese brothers and the run-in with Mr. Wu's drug operations.

All of these things seemed like a string of odd events that didn't fit with each other. Ahmad laughed softly. "No one knows what will happen to them," he whispered.

He began drifting off to sleep, Allah knows his muscles ached enough to put ten men to bed for a week! As he floated away on the ocean of dreams, he recalled the riddle of the old man: *When the sign of good is in his hand.* What did that mean? Then, he remembered his wonderful time in the Masjid: the brothers, the fragrent gardens and the colors splashed like rainbows over the high walls of the prayer area.

He felt again the sadness of having to leave and how the brothers smiled at him...*and how the older Muslim handed him something.*

"When the sign of good is in his hand."

A book! The brother handed him a book!

Instantly, Ahmad came out of his drowsy slumber and remembered that the brother had given him a farewell gift, a book. What was it? He hadn't even looked at it yet. It was still in his jacket pocket. Curiosity animated his tired limbs as he dragged himself to his feet and took his jacket in his hands.

After fumbling through the pockets, he pulled out the small book and took it with him back to his mat. He sat down and studied the cover. There was only one Chinese symbol adorning the front cover of the book. What did it mean? Ahmad took out his China book and looked the symbol up in the glossary section at the back. After searching for a moment he found the definition. This symbol stood for—-*Eternity, Forever.*

"Odd." Thought Ahmad. "What kind of book talks about *forever?*"

When he opened up the book and flipped through the pages, he smiled as wide as he possibly could. What the brother had given him *indeed* talks about forever.

"By the Time, Verily humans are in a state of loss, except those who believe and do good and who teach each other truth and patience." The brother gave him a Qur'an with the Arabic text and the Chinese translation! "The sign of *good* in his hand!" He exclaimed.

"The sign of good is *the Qur'an!*"

Ahmad was elated. "*Allahu Akbar,*" he yelled in triumph. He still didn't know how a Qur'an would help in the struggle ahead, but he was certain of one thing: there wasn't any better sign than this to boost his spirits. When his excitement died down a bit, he returned to his mat and opened the book up to read. Although he couldn't read Chinese, he could read the Arabic. He could understand a lot of the words too.

The chapter he opened to, quite by accident, was called *The Jinn*. As he started reading, he began to get ideas, and a rush of insight and understanding flooded his mind. He did not sleep until many hours later.

18

Ahmad woke up the next morning for prayers and afterward asked Allah to give him strength in the coming confrontation. He felt stronger now than he had ever felt in his life, but he still was unsure of himself. Although he trained hard for over a week with martial arts masters, he realized there was still so much to learn.

Shang Dao told him that everything was going to happen this very night: the rescue of Stickman, the showdown with Xandar Kul. But Mr. Wu was here also. How would that fit into the picture?

Ahmad wasted no time in thinking further. He didn't need anything to make him feel more nervous. Instead, he decided to practice some of what he learned. Maybe a good work-out would ease his troubled mind.

He left his room and went to Master Yu's training room. Of course, Yu wasn't there because it was early yet. Ahmad walked to the center of the large, empty chamber and started to do some warm-up stretches and exercises he had learned. After a few minutes, he shook out his arms and legs to loosen up and then prepared to do a Shaolin Long-Fist form.

He relaxed his breathing and then raised both hands to his waist his front of him. He stepped forward with his right foot and then let loose a fast kick with his left. Turning to the right he bent forward and shot both his arms out in fists through the air.

As he continued with the movements of the form, his mind began to drift off in thought. He still executed each part of the form exactly as he learned it from Master Yu, but his focus, his mind was elsewhere. What had he read last night in the book he was given?

Declare, "It has been revealed to me that a group of jinn came and heard (this Qur'an)." The jinn had said, 'What a great reading we just heard! It gives guidance to the right and so now we believe in it. We will never add anything to the (worship) of our Lord again! Certainly, high is the majesty of our Lord and he doesn't have a wife or son.

'There are some foolish (jinn) among us who say terrible lies against Allah; but we think that no human or jinn should say anything untrue against Allah. It is true that some humans call upon some of us Jinn for safety, but the humans only make great mistakes.'"

When Ahmad came out of his day-dreaming, he found that he had just completed a perfect form. He was breathing heavy from the exertion and beads of sweat collected on his forehead. When he relaxed his body again, he thought to himself how glad he was his dad made him learn the language of the Qur'an. He was also pleased at a form well done.

"Excellent!" a hidden voice announced. "You have learned the form well."

Ahmad looked around him and saw Master Yu step out of the shadows towards him. "You have learned the form and many fighting techniques from it."

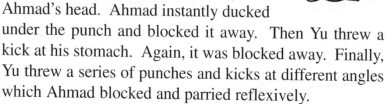

When Yu stood before Ahmad, he suddenly thrust out his fist straight at Ahmad's head. Ahmad instantly ducked under the punch and blocked it away. Then Yu threw a kick at his stomach. Again, it was blocked away. Finally, Yu threw a series of punches and kicks at different angles which Ahmad blocked and parried reflexively.

"Good," said Master Yu. "You are well on your way to becoming a warrior."

Ahmad thanked Master Yu for being his instructor and then retreated from the chamber towards Master Fong's battle-practice room. When he reached the door and pushed it open, he found the room dark and unoccupied. "So much the better," thought Ahmad.

He looked around at the many wooden poles scattered about the room. Each one would spin and only stop when a special button was hit on it. The wooden arms were not attached but were, rather, stacked up in a corner.

Ahmad went over to the wooden arms and grabbed a handful. Carefully, he attached the arms to the poles. When he was through, he found the lever that started the poles spinning. He flicked it on and then looked across the dimly-lit room.

Each pole was spinning. The wooden arms turned with the pole creating a potential danger for anyone who came too near. Ahmad practiced this a few times in good light, now he wanted to do it in the shadows. He steadied his breathing and then yelled, "*Hiiiiyaaa!*" as he charged straight into the middle of the poles.

Ahmad ducked when a wooden arm came at his face, but another one hit him in the shoulder. Ahmad blocked one rushing furiously at his leg but got whacked by one on his back. Ahmad rolled forward on the floor and kicked up at a pole. Bingo! He hit the button and that pole stopped. He rushed at the other poles, arms whirling and struck until he stopped another, and another, until finally all the poles lay still.

Ahmad rose from his last fighting stance, sweating buckets and breathing heavy. He smiled as he rubbed his bruises and aching muscles.

"You have learned well." A voice announced.

Ahmad turned to see Masters Fong and Lui standing in the door. Master Fong walked to a lamp and lit it causing light to invade the darkened room.

"He is certainly stronger and more ready than when he arrived." Lui said to Fong.

"Yes, indeed." Master Fong replied.

Ahmad thanked his teachers who smiled with pride and then left to take a much needed bath. When he had finished, he changed his clothes and returned to his room. There he found Shang Dao sitting in a chair, along with the usual tray of food.

"I hope your work-out went well," he said to Ahmad.

"Yes, it was good."

"Now, we must discuss tonight. Are you still sure you want to go through with this?"

Ahmad, knowing that Stickman's life depended on him, nodded his head and said, "Yes, I'm sure."

"Then sit here, for I will tell you what you must do."

Ahmad took a seat near Shang Dao and listened intently to the instructions. After half an hour passed, Shang Dao left so that Ahmad could rest a few hours before night came.

Ahmad dozed and refreshed his tired body. When the sun finally set, Ahmad was already awake and preparing himself for what he must do.

19

Ahmad crept down the deserted hallway as quietly as he could. He was heading towards the part of the temple controlled by the drug-dealers. That was where Stickman was being held. That also was where Mr. Wu and the jinn named Xandar Kul lurked. Ahmad had to move carefully.

Shang Dao told him where to find Stickman, and he also said that no monk could go with him because the jinn had cast some kind of fear spell over them, preventing them from using their Kung-Fu abilities to fight back.

Ahmad walked for a few more yards, his shoes barely making a sound on the stone floor. He came upon a stairway going down. Mr. Wu's drug operation was down there somewhere. Shang Dao said there would be guards on duty- and maybe even worse. A spirit creature like Xandar Kul could call upon all sorts of evil if it wanted to.

It was well past midnight, Ahmad thought, so maybe the guards would be asleep and this rescue would be a snap.

At least that's what he hoped. After tugging his jacket around himself more closely, Ahmad moved down the stairs, one step at a time.

When he reached the bottom, he entered a passageway leading to the left or to the right. Shang Dao said Stickman would be in a cell down the hallway leading to the left. The drug labs and storage areas were down the other way. After making sure the coast was clear, Ahmad walked silently down the left passageway.

He passed a few doors on the left and right of him. Shang Dao said it would be the seventh door on the right. As he neared the seventh door, Ahmad walked more confidently, thinking that this was going to be a piece of cake.

Suddenly, Ahmad's foot hit something which nearly sent him sprawling. He looked down in time to just barely catch a glimpse of a small, lizard-like creature maybe two feet in length. It was partially hidden in the shadows and when Ahmad tried to get a closer look it hissed and scampered back down the hall. *"Strange,"* Ahmad thought. "I hope, whatever it was, stays gone."

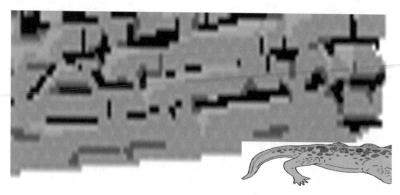

After steadying himself, Ahmad approached the seventh door and looked for a way to open it. A heavy iron latch secured it in place so that no one could ever hope to open it from the inside. Ahmad set his flickering lantern on the ground and then lifted the rusty handle. After a moment's struggle, he moved the latch to the unlock position.

Taking a deep breath, he whispered, "*Bismillah,*" "*In the Name of Allah,*" and slowly pushed the door inward. The room was dark and the sparse light from the hallway barely made it possible to see. When Ahmad's eyes adjusted to the dimness, he could see a figure in one corner, hunched over as if asleep.

Ahmad moved to the figure and saw that it was Stickman. He gently nudged his shoulder and whispered loudly, "*Stickman! Stickman, get up.*"

Stickman moved a little but then kept sleeping. He started to snore. Ahmad shook him more firmly this time, repeating the command. Slowly, Stickman regained consciousness. When he saw someone standing over him he started to cry out, "***Please***, let me out of here. I won't tell nobody. I promise."

Ahmad looked down at the pathetic Stickman. His clothes were dirty, his face was dirty and he looked as if he hadn't eaten very well in several days. "Stickman," Ahmad said, "it's me, Ahmad. Ahmad Deen, your room-mate. Remember?"

Stickman blinked hard and sat quiet for half a second. Then, his eyes went wide and he started yelling,

"Deen, you gotta get me outta here! They're gonna kill me! I saw Mr. Wu go into a secret door, and I saw some drugs. They beat me up and brought me here. They said they're gonna teach me a lesson and then *kill me*...."

Stickman would have probably continued yelling if Ahmad hadn't have slapped his face and covered his mouth. "*Quiet you idiot*," he scolded. "*Do you want to attract every guard in the place?*"

Stickman, who was startled by Ahmad's action, relaxed and quieted himself down. "How did you get here?" he asked in hushed tones.

"It's a long story," replied Ahmad. "Let's just get out of here, and I'll tell you later. Now you have to do everything I say. Got it?"

Stickman nodded, and Ahmad helped him get to his feet and then moved him to the open door of the cell. After checking to make sure the coast was clear, Ahmad pulled Stickman along with him, retracing the way he came. This was too easy.

Then it happened: as they were passing by one of those doors in the hall, a huge sheet of stone came crashing down in front of them, cutting off the way ahead of them. When they turned around to head the other way, another sheet of stone slid down sealing them in between. "*Aaaaah!*" screamed Stickman.

Ahmad pushed against the stone as hard as he could. Stickman panicked and started pounding at the walls. Nothing budged. Those stone walls weren't going anywhere.

Then, with a slight creak, the door that they had been passing by, opened inward. Ahmad looked at Stickman, then at the door. "Are we supposed to go in there?" whined Stickman.

Before he could answer, the walls began to shake. Then, the two slabs of stone started moving towards each other. Realizing that if they stayed there they would be crushed, Ahmad yelled, "I think so!"

Then he grabbed Stickman, and they plunged through the open door just before the stone slabs collided together in a loud "**Bam!**"

Ahmad and Stickman looked behind them and watched in amazement as the slabs began to shiver before vanishing into thin air. Before they could react, however, the door slammed shut, locking them inside.

"*Heh, heh, heh,*" a voice laughed. "You foolish boys. Falling for a simple *illusion.*"

When the pair turned to face whoever was in there with them, they were shocked in silence at the strange man they saw. Ahead of them, seated on a large wooden chair, sat a huge muscle-man, who had skin that looked muddy-red.

His head was bald, except for a huge helmet, and he wore a large cape. His face was hideous to look upon and his lips curled in an evil snarl. Next to him, curled up around his leg, was a small lizard-like creature, that had a curiously human-like head.

"Now I have two victims to toy with, *Ikhsa,*" the man said as he bent down to stroke the creature's head. It

hissed in pleasure and opened its mouth, exposing little sharp, nasty teeth.

Ahmad rose to his feet, trembling, while Stickman fell to the floor and cowered in fear.

"You must be *Xandar Kul*," Ahmad said in a shaky voice."

"I am, *puny human*," Xandar replied. "How dare you enter this place. Who do you think you are?"

"*That*," a new voice called out, "is the stupid boy who brought the police to one of my drug hide-outs."

Ahmad blinked in disbelief as Mr. Wu entered the room from a door nearby where the Jinn sat. "And now I will have you both pay for the trouble you have caused me."

Stickman cried out, "It's not my fault. I promise I won't tell anyone. I promise!"

"I will enjoy watching you both die," Mr. Wu said elatedly. "Xandar Kul," he ordered, "*kill them both!*"

Xandar rose from his chair and attained his full height of seven feet. The muscles rippled across his reddish chest, and a devilish grin came upon his lips. "Yes, *master*," he replied as he eyed the two boys menacingly. "It will be a *brutal* pleasure."

He started to walk towards Ahmad and Stickman. He waved his right arm in the air and instantly a long, curved sword and shield appeared in his hands. "Prepare to die!" he boomed.

Stickman screamed in terror and ran back to the closed door behind him, scratching and clawing to get out. Ahmad looked to the right and left: no way to escape! The giant reached him and raised his sword above his head. He brought it down straight at Ahmad who barely managed to jump out the way. The sword hit the stone floor with a loud *"Claang."*

The giant appeared annoyed and looked behind him to see where Ahmad ran. Then, he noticed Stickman and decided to strike down the easier target first. Stickman looked up at the sword coming down on him and yelled, *"Noooooo! Heeelp me! Aaaaaaah!"*

Just as the giant was about to slice the boy in half, Ahmad leapt towards him with a flying kick and struck Xandar in the back. His sword missed Stickman and cut a deep gash in the wooden door.

Stickman scrambled to the side and shivered helplessly. Meanwhile, the enraged jinn bellowed out in anger, "How dare you strike me, human!"

Xandar flung himself after Ahmad who ducked behind the wooden chair. Mr. Wu laughed from the corner he was standing in, "Finally, Xandar," he called out. "Some challenge for you. That makes it all the more enjoyable."

    "*You are dead, human!*" Xandar screamed at Ahmad. Then, the jinn raised his shield arm and hit the wooden chair with all his force. The wood splintered in a thousand pieces, sending Ahmad reeling backwards.

Ahmad crashed into the wall behind him and slid to the floor. A nasty bruise covered both his shoulders and he ached all over his body. He barely managed to run before the slower moving giant reached him. He ducked behind a small table and shouted, "Allah made humans better than jinns!"

"No!" cried Xandar, "We are made from fire! We are better!" He swung his sword sideways and almost chopped the table's legs, and Ahmad, in half, but Ahmad rolled forward on the floor and then kicked Xandar in the knee cap. There was a loud 'snapping' sound and Ahmad rolled away to the side.

The giant squealed in pain and reached for his hurt knee. He put his foot on the floor, took a step, then stumbled. He couldn't walk right! **"You will pay!"** he cried.

Ahmad jumped back from another swing which nearly caught his arm. Then, when Xandar seemed exhausted, Ahmad sprung his trap. He pulled out his Qur'an from his jacket and called to the giant who was breathing heavily by the wall. "Hey, Xandar!"

The jinn looked up as steam was coming from his forehead. He seemed to grow in size. Ahmad had to make his move fast.

"Have you heard of this book?" Ahmad asked. "It's a Qur'an. The smart jinn have already accepted what it says."

Xandar almost dropped his sword in surprise.

Then, Ahmad recited a chapter from the Qur'an that translates into English like this:

In the Name of Allah,
the Compassionate Source of All Mercy.

Declare, "I seek safety with the Lord of people, the King of people, the God of people, from the trouble of the slinking whisperer who whispers (fear) into the hearts of people, whether they are from among the jinn or other people."

Xandar stared ahead in disbelief. He dropped his sword with a loud metallic clank and said something in a strange language. When Mr. Wu saw the jinn standing still he called out in anger, "Xandar! Do what you are ordered! *Kill them!*"

Xandar turned slowly to face Mr. Wu. He locked eyes with the drug boss and said coldly, "This was not in our bargain. You did not tell me I would face one of the believers in Allah. He chanted the Surah of protection. I am powerless against him now. **Enough!**"

Then, Xandar's reddish color changed to yellow, then blue, then white and finally with a flash of light, he vanished in a spectacular explosion.

The room became silent. Mr. Wu looked on in shock. He turned and ran out the door he came from. Ahmad and Stickman were alone.

Ahmad stood shocked for a second. *"It worked! It really worked!"* He thought. Then he came back to his senses when he heard Stickman groaning behind him. "Get me outta here!" He whined weakly. His voice sounded hoarse from all the crying and screaming.

Ahmad lifted him up and opened the door leading back into the hallway. When they reached the stairs they climbed quickly and jogged to the exit doors. They reached the way out of the main temple building after a few minutes and rushed out into the open. It was no longer night as the coming dawn cast its light upon the horizon.

As fast as he could, Ahmad dragged Stickman after him and made his way to the main entrance of the Shaolin monastery. Once they were clear of the main gates, they would be home free!

The pair rounded the last corner leading to the front gates when they saw something that made them stop in their tracks. Twenty feet ahead of them, blocking the way out, stood Mr. Wu! Behind him were all the guards from the whole drug operation. There must have been forty of them in all. Each one held weapons ranging from knives, to chains, to clubs. Mr. Wu held a handgun and had a stern look in his eyes.

"Going somewhere?" He called out. "I think not! You have caused far too much trouble for me to just let you get away like that."

Mr. Wu then raised the gun and pointed it at Ahmad. "Who should I kill first?" He asked with a devilish grin.

"You'll never get away with this." Ahmad declared.

Stickman crouched back down on his knees and cried and wailed.

"That decides it," Mr. Wu said casually.

But before he could fire the gun at Stickman, Shang Dao came out of nowhere and threw a metal star at Wu's hand. The biting edges of the weapon sank deep in his wrist causing him to drop the gun harmlessly to the ground.

Mr. Wu screamed in pain and looked at the monk with hatred in his eyes.

"Your evil spirit is gone," Shang Dao yelled loudly. "The fear to fight you has left us. You are finished here. You may leave now and never return, or you will face the consequences of Shaolin justice."

Mr. Wu's face contorted and shivered in rage. A red angry color flooded his cheeks as he held the wound on his wrist. "I will have my men kill you and tear you to bits! What can one old man do to save himself from that?"

Shang Dao smiled slightly and waved his arm once. A second later, dozens of Shaolin monks came out from behind buildings and out of doorways. Their yellow and orange robes flowing swiftly with every step. The monks arranged themselves behind Shang Dao and waited silently.

Stickman and Ahmad, who were in the middle of these two opposing groups, looked around themselves warily. Mr. Wu cried out in an angry fit to his men, "*Get them! Kill them all!*"

Instantly, his thugs raised their weapons and rushed at the monks yelling battle cries and curses. Ahmad pulled Stickman to his feet and ran as fast as he could towards the safety of Shang Dao and the monks. Shang Dao waited until the raging drug dealers covered half the distance then he raised his hand and signaled for the monks to engage.

As if one wall, the monks surged forward to meet the enemy that had humiliated them for so long. They passed Ahmad and Stickman running full speed at the thugs, yelling battle cries of their own.

When Ahmad reached Shang Dao, he and Stickman turned to watch the ferocious battle behind them. It seemed as if it were a dream to Ahmad. Orange and yellow robes moved like ocean waves through the black and gray clothes of the criminals.

Fists were bashing, weapons flew, kicks were thrown out in all directions and men seemed to fly this way and that.

Three drug-men surrounded Master Chai and jumped him. Ahmad began to shout a warning, but Chai merely swung his strong arms out sending his attackers reeling. Then, Ahmad saw Master Fong. He was dodging the knife-thrusts of several men and kicking and punching ferociously.

Other monks pulled out weapons made of steel and wood and drove at the criminals furiously. One monk wielded a three-sectional staff and was hitting the daggers and knives out of all who came near. Another monk had a long chain-whip which he swung at the enemy, tangling it around their arms and dragging them to the ground. Once there, he finished them off with a strike from his free hand.

The monks, who had superior Kung-Fu skills, eventually were able to disarm all of the thugs. The hand-to- hand fighting that followed, however, was fierce. The drug-men knew this was a struggle for their survival. The wounded and unconscious fell one after another. Some were monks, others criminals.

Ahmad turned around to see Master Yu thrashing two guards fiercely. "What style is that?" Ahmad asked, almost hypnotized.

"That's *Tiger style*," responded Shang Dao.

Time after time, Master Yu's '*claws*' left the helpless thugs with shredded uniforms and skin. Ahmad and Stickman watched in silent fascination. The full battle must have lasted over half an hour!

But in the end, the outnumbered, yet tougher monks, managed to take down all the drug dealers, who lay in pain on the ground. When the last man was subdued, the monks took ropes and cords and tied the hands of all the criminals.

They were lined up like prisoners and made to sit on the ground silently. A monk walked over to Mr. Wu and wrapped a cloth around his wound. Wu looked up in disbelief at the help he was getting. Then, he lowered his head in shame.

Ahmad was wonder-struck by all that he just witnessed. "Such fighting power," he whispered under his breath.

"Yes," Shang Dao replied, "training and skill are what make a man a fighter, but a heart free from evil makes a man a warrior."

Ahmad nodded in understanding. He grew inside. He knew it. "*Alhumdulillah.*" He said.

Stickman groaned on the ground, "Oooooh. Does anyone got any food?"

Ahmad laughed and Shang Dao joined in. "You will have all you need to eat. But first, you will need a bath!"

Stickman looked at his dirty clothes and laughed aloud also. It felt good to laugh after being locked up by drug criminals. Ahmad picked Stickman up to his feet and led him inside to the room with the bathing pool. Meanwhile, Shang Dao went to call the police. Justice would come to all who did wrong in the end.

20

"*Ahmad Deen!*" Ms. Morris called out from behind the door. "Open up! We're back."

Ahmad opened the door to see Ms. Morris and a few of the other students standing nearby. They each held bags stuffed with souvenirs and wore pink hats that read, "*I saw the Great Wall.*"

"Just thought you'd like to know that the trip was very exciting." She said. Then, she peered into the room to see Stickman sitting on his bed. Papers and pens were scattered around him. "Oh, I see Brian was finally found. Did Mr. Wu have much trouble finding him?"

"Uh, no," Ahmad replied. "He found him very quickly, actually."

"Good. I knew he would."

"We were just working on the report you gave us to do. I'm sorry we're not finished yet," Stickman called out to her.

"Well," she mused. "I feel really bad that you two missed such a wonderful time. The Great Wall was magnificent. After ten days we couldn't even see everything there. Don't worry about the report boys. I'll let it slide this time. Missing the rest of the trip is punishment enough."

Ahmad and Stickman let out a sigh of relief. Not only did Ms. Morris *not* know they just got back to the hotel an hour before, but they didn't have to do that long report either. "All right!" the two exclaimed in unison.

"But I do hope this escapade of yours will teach you a lesson." she continued, "If you don't follow the rules, you'll have no fun."

Ahmad and Stickman looked at each other and grimaced. "Yes, Ms. Morris," answered Ahmad. "We learned our lesson."

"Good. Now just so you don't feel *too* bad, I brought a present for each of you." She reached into her bag and pulled out two sealed envelopes. She handed them to Ahmad and said, "Here, give one to Brian."

Ahmad took them and passed one over to Stickman who had just stood up from his bed.

"Now, we're leaving tonight at eight o'clock sharp. Pack your bags and be ready to go to the airport when I call." Then, Ms. Morris turned around and left.

Ahmad closed the door and Stickman held up his hand in a high five. Ahmad slapped his hand eagerly and then returned to sit at the edge of his bed.

"Do you think we should tell her what happened to us?" asked Stickman.

"*Naah!*" replied Ahmad. "She wouldn't believe us anyway." Then, Ahmad picked up his pillow and threw it at Stickman saying, "All I know is that I missed a trip to the Great Wall because of you."

Stickman laughed and threw the pillow back saying, "And I missed a lot of good dinners waiting for you to come and get me!"

Later, on the plane flight back home, Ahmad thought about everything that happened to him. The mystery, the danger, the friends he made and the skills he learned. But what he cherished most of all was the courage he found within himself to stand up tall, even in the face of the greatest danger.

Next to him, Stickman was dozing quietly. For some reason he wasn't getting plane-sick this time. He probably grew a little inside too, thought Ahmad. He looked out the window at the clouds drifting by like giant ships. He would never forget this trip.

He reached into his coat pocket and pulled out the envelope Ms. Morris gave him. He unsealed it and pulled out a photograph that made him smile. He looked at it and studied it with delight. He may not have had the chance to see it in person, but Ms. Morris made sure that he could take at least something of it home. It was a picture of the Great Wall of China.

Ahmad studied it a moment longer, before leaning his head back. Boy, would he have a tale to tell his younger sister, Layla, when he got home. If she would ever believe him! This time, the flight didn't seem so long.

Selected Titles Available From IBTS

Layla Deen and the Case of the Ramadan Rogue

By Yahiya Emerick

Somebody's trying to ruin her Ramadan! Layla Deen and her family were just settling in to break a long days fast when their mother came running from the kitchen and cried, *"Someone stole the food for Iftar!"* Layla knew it was a terrible crime and decided to get to the bottom of this mystery. See what happens! Illustrated. 54 pages.

Ahmad Deen and the Curse of the Aztec Warrior

By Yahiya Emerick

Where is he? Ahmad Deen and his sister Layla thought they were getting a nice vacation in tropical Mexico. But what they're really going to get is a hair-raising race against time to save their father from becoming the next victim of an ancient, bloody ritual!

How can Ahmad save his father *and* deal with his bratty sister at the same time? To make matters worse, no one seems to want to help them find the mysterious lost city that may hold the key to their father's whereabouts. And then there's that jungle guide with the strangely familiar jacket. Are they brave enough—or crazy enough, to take on the *Curse of the Aztec Warrior?* Illustrated, 64 pages.

Isabella: A Girl of Muslim Spain

By Yahiya Emerick

A classic tale about a young girl who finds Islam, and danger, amidst the harrowing religious conflicts of medieval Muslim Spain.

Experience firsthand what life was like in the splendid Muslim city of Cordoba. See through the eyes of Isabella as she struggles with her father's Christian beliefs and finds that life is not always as easy as people think. Embark on a journey into history, into the heart, as you follow her path from darkness into light.

Highly recommended for teenagers and young adults. A sensitive and realistic portrayal from a unique point of view unlike anything you have ever read. Illustrated, 128 pages.

The Army of Lions

By Qasim Najar

Get ready for swashbuckling and deeds of valor at its finest! The Army of Lions is coming! Take yourself back to the days when a believer and his faith could destroy every evil tyrant, when the brave and true could sweep over the plains and cities of the world and make them take notice. If you're impressed by unswerving determination and faith that conquers all, then be prepared to join the Army of Lions! A full length fiction novel set in the golden age of Islam. Illustrated, 178 pages.

The Memory of Hands

By Reshma Baig

A collection of short stories centering on the lives of Muslims in urban America and overseas. An exploration of the experiences of the Muslim Diaspora. A poetic journey which ventures to understand the phenomena of cultural and spiritual transplantation from the perspective of American Muslim voices. The stories examine the plethora of conflicts which emerge when a cultural tradition, which is not always based on Islam, is brought to the American landscape: a new land where neither one's original culture nor Islam has roots. Excellent reading material. Probably the first true literature meant for Muslims, written by a Muslim, in the tradition of the great authors of the literary genre. 158 pages.

Muslim Youth Speak: Voices of Today's Young Muslims

Edited by Yahiya Emerick

What do Muslim youth today think about Islam? What are their suggestions for living and promoting it? What are their observations about the state of Islam in America today and how to make it grow? This book is a compilation of essays, plays, prose and other writings by actual Muslim youth. Find out what's going on in the minds of the second generation! Book, 156 pages.